Waybuloo

De Li
and the Strawberries

EGMONT
We bring stories to life

First published in Great Britain 2009 by Egmont UK Limited
239 Kensington High Street, London W8 6SA
Waybuloo ™ & © 2009 The Foundation
TV Productions Limited/Decode/Blue Entertainment.
Licensed by RDF Rights. All rights reserved.
With the support of the MEDIA Programme of the European Union.

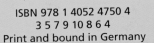

ISBN 978 1 4052 4750 4
3 5 7 9 10 8 6 4
Print and bound in Germany

FSC
Mixed Sources
Product group from well-managed
forests and other controlled sources
Cert no. TT-COC-002332
www.fsc.org
© 1996 Forest Stewardship Council

Egmont is passionate about helping to preserve the world's remaining ancient forests.
We only use paper from legal and sustainable forest sources.

This book is made from paper certified by the Forestry Stewardship Council (FSC),
an organisation dedicated to promoting responsible management of forest resources.
For more information on the FSC, please visit www.fsc.org. To learn more about
Egmont's sustainable paper policy, please visit www.egmont.co.uk/ethical

De Li and her narabug have found
something special on their walk . . .

"Strawberries! De Li's favourite!"
smiles De Li.

She picks a juicy strawberry from the bush
and takes a bite.

"Buloo!" she smiles, floating up into the air.

De Li fetches her basket and picks strawberries for everyone!

She shares them with her Pipling friends, Lau Lau, Nok Tok and Yojojo.

"Thank you, De Li!" they say. The strawberries taste delicious.

But what's that noise? It's the cheebies!

"Let's play peeka!" says De Li.
"Piplings hide!"

The Piplings look for a place to hide,
before the cheebies arrive.

Yojojo hides behind the log! De Li hides
behind the bush!

"Lau Lau help Nok Tok," says Lau Lau.
She hides Nok Tok behind the rock.

Playing peeka makes Lau Lau happy.
"Buloo!" she smiles.

She floats up into the sky and finds a hiding place in the tree with her narabug.

Soon the cheebies find all four Piplings.
"Hooray!" they cheer.

De Li wants to share the strawberries with the cheebies.

But, oh dear, De Li's basket is empty. **"Strawberries all gone!"** says De Li.

The cheebies will have to help her pick some more.

"Let's all look for strawberries!" says Yojojo.

De Li fetches more baskets from her house so the Piplings and the cheebies can pick strawberries together.

De Li's narabug has come to help, too!

"Come on, cheebies. This way!"
says Nok Tok.

The cheebies follow Nok Tok. Over
the hill . . . through the trees . . . and
down the path until they reach . . .

. . . the strawberry bush!

"Hooray!" cheer the cheebies.

Nok Tok, Yojojo and Lau Lau help the cheebies pick lots of juicy strawberries. Soon their baskets are full!

But where is De Li? She's forgotten the way to the strawberry bush!

De Li's narabug knows the way! But when they reach the bush, there is only one strawberry left.

"One strawberry not enough for everyone!" cries De Li.

De Li's clever narabug can smell more strawberries! It flutters off to find them.

De Li follows her narabug to find the strawberries.

The Piplings and the cheebies are waiting for De Li, with enough strawberries for everyone!

"Surprise!" the Piplings and the cheebies say together.

"Piplings and cheebies pick for De Li!" says Yojojo proudly.

De Li is happy. **"Now everyone has strawberries!"** she smiles.

She floats up, up into the air. **"Buloo!"** says De Li.

Nok Tok, Lau Lau and
Yojojo begin to float too.

"Waybuloo!" they
say together.
**"Bye bye, cheebies.
See you soon!"**